DEEPER

BAD BOYS OF TEXAS, BOOK 3

TORY BAKER

Copyright © 2021 by Tory Baker

All rights reserved. No part of this book may be reproduced in any form or by any electronic or mechanical means, including information storage and retrieval systems, without written permission from the author, except for the use of brief quotations in a book review.

Please respect the author and do not participate in or encourage piracy of copyrighted materials that would violate the author's rights.

This is a work of fiction. Names, characters, businesses, places, events, locales, and incidents are either the products of the author's imagination or used in a fictitious manner. Any resemblance to actual persons, living or dead, or actual events is purely coincidental.

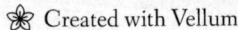 Created with Vellum

No matter how educated, talented, rich or cool you believe you are, how you treat people ultimately tells all. Integrity is everything.- Unkown

PROLOGUE
REESE

THANK goodness it's summer and I don't have to think about lesson plans, my classroom, or the ridiculousness that comes with working in the elite of super-elite private schools for the lifestyle of the rich and famous. That's why I did something I have never done before, even my friends thought I was crazy. A single woman going off for the summer, renting a small cottage in the town of Galveston, Texas. It's only a couple of hours from where I work. Sadly, as much as I love teaching and the children involved, I loathe the faculty. And don't get me started on the parents. Sometimes I think they expect their children to piss excellence even when they're already at the top of their class.

That's another reason I'm getting away. Burnout is real, and it's time for me to re-evaluate this career path I'm on and if I'd rather change schools or jobs.

"Holy shit," I breathe out, interrupting my own thoughts. I've just walked into a bar here in Galveston, not at all what I was expecting. It's dark and moody, neon lights above where the barstools are announcing 'Wolf's Bar and Grill'. The country music clear from the eighties is playing, people are line dancing, and shots are being slung back like its water. My own body sways to the rhythm of the sultry music playing of none other than the king of country music, George Strait. I make my way to where everyone is line dancing and join in. Not caring that I'm wearing the most unconventional shoes as we do a box-style dance. By the time the song is over, I'm parched, sweat is gathering at the nape of my neck and traveling down towards my chest. I'm fanning myself as I walk off the dance floor when I'm stopped in my tracks. There's a man in a black Stetson cowboy hat walking my way, well, not really, but to where I'm placing my rear end after that dance. Me, the girl who's here by herself, wearing a white tank top, distressed cut-off jean shorts, and flip flops. I'm clearly not dressed for this bar, but I couldn't help but walk in to see what it was about. I'm sure glad I did too. I make my way towards the man whose eyes haven't left mine. The bar isn't overly busy, and I'm thankful as I slide onto a stool.

"How can I help you, sunshine?" the handsome hunk of a man asks me in a deep Southern drawl, and I'm gobsmacked, struck quiet, and words are seriously hard. That's probably why I'm taking my time staring at him from head to toe. He's got longish brown hair that is peeping out at the nape of his collar, dark skin, a sharp jawline, and hauntingly pretty blue eyes that I can see even in the smoky haze that's filling the room. His smile though, it's as if he knows what he's got going on and he's not afraid to turn on the charm. This cowboy most definitely has trouble written all over him, and I'm more than ready to see just what kind I can get into.

"Sex on the Beach, please?" I return with a smile that's probably ridiculously goofy.

"You got it." He taps the bar top with his hands, showing off his muscular arms that are encased in a tight black shirt with the bar's name emblazoned on it, and when he turns around... shew, the way this cowboy can fill out a pair of jeans, I do believe I'm in for a good time.

ONE

WOLF

I MAKE the vixen the drink she requested, making sure to give her an eyeful of my arms. With how she was eye fucking them, I knew it'd be something she'd enjoy, plus seeing the apples of her cheeks bloom with pinkness had me thinking all kinds of crazy thoughts. The way she was shaking her ass on the dance floor, not even seeing the way people made room for her as she kept up with the other dancers. My eyes never left her body, that's for fucking sure.

"Can anyone ride the mechanical bull?" Dark mocha hair with shots of caramel, porcelain-white skin, green eyes that can see deep into your soul, and lips that were meant for kissing. Already looking bee stung and ripe for my own, red in color, and I'd love to see just what else matches the color of her lips.

"Yeah, you want to ride it?" I turn around, bringing the drink she ordered to the bar top.

"Maybe not tonight. I don't think I'm dressed for the occasion." She holds up her foot to show me her shoes, making my mouth salivate at her legs and how flexible she is.

"I guess it's a good thing I'm here most nights in case you want to ride Bushwhacker." The way she lets her laugh out, abandoning any kind of pretense of modesty, has other men near the bar looking at her. I'm no idiot. I stand up straight, my arms crossed over my chest, and let them know to back the fuck off.

"Oh my, is that really its name? I mean, surely, with a name like that it has men and women laughing the entire time they attempt to hold on." I watch the way her tongue chases after the straw until she finds it, sucking it like her life depends on it.

"That's really the name, brought it down here from my hometown where bull riders would use it as practice. Stick around long enough and you'll see some real entertainment. I'm Wolf, by the way." I hold my hand out to hers.

"Reese, and I think I just might. I'm assuming this place is yours, considering your name." The smile she gives me along with her small, much daintier hand engulfed in mine that's riddled with callouses from work is a contradiction, but the way my body reacts to hers, I know that there's no way I'll let this woman leave tonight without me at least getting her phone number.

"You let me know when you need another one. I'm going to see if those guys over there need a fresh beer." Letting her know I'm not going anywhere, not if I can help it.

"Oh, let me pay you, in case you get busy and I wander around?" She moves to grab her wallet out of her purse that's hanging across her body, highlighting the size of her tits.

"I'll show you around. Give me a few minutes, and don't worry about the drink." She settles down, and that's when I make my way through the rest of the patrons at the bar. Since it's the middle of the week, we aren't too busy yet. That will change come the weekend, and that's usually when I'll let the bartenders I've hired work the crowds to bring in their money. I utilize that time to take care of the books, order alcohol, and then help out if the crowd gets out of control. Which seems to happen the busier we get into tourist season. One thing I'm banking on now is that Reese will give me the opportunity to do a whole lot more than show her around.

TWO

REESE

THE GOOSE BUMPS that pebbled up on top of my skin still haven't gone down since Wolf's touch more than a few minutes ago. It probably doesn't help that every time I try to be nonchalant, he catches me in the act of gazing at him.

"Aren't you a pretty girl." A woman takes the barstool next to me. My head whips around. A smile graces her face, short brown hair cut in a bob and blue eyes that sparkle with mischief.

"Me?" I ask, looking around while pointing to myself.

"Of course, you. I'm Julia. That's my boy over there. I couldn't be prouder of him. Not with the way I upped and moved, he didn't bat an eye, just followed my move. Busted his tail until he scrimped and saved every penny working on any rodeo he could that was within driving distance, squirreled away that money. And when Mr. McKinley was ready to sell this place, Wolf paid cash for it." She offers up this information freely, though it leaves me reeling. As if I'm an outsider and learned this in a way I probably shouldn't have.

"Wow," I breathe out, because I'm astonished. Wolf can't be much older than me, and I'm twenty-five.

"Hey, Ma." The man of the hour leans over the bar top, giving his mom a kiss on the cheek.

"Fancy seeing you here. Kind of slowing tonight, hmm?" She hands him a bag with what looks like Tupperware inside it.

"It's only Wednesday, always a slow night when I'm working the bar. You know that. I see you've met Reese." He nods in my direction, a grin showing off his perfectly straight teeth along with a dimple on the right side of his cheek.

"I should have put two and two together, the eyes, the hair. You two are clones." I move to where I'm brokering the corner of my seat to watch the go-between with these two.

"It's a pleasure to meet you, Reese. Since, you know, my boy here has seemingly lost his manners. Are you new here?" she asks while shaking my hand.

"Reese Miller. I'm here for the summer. The perk of being a schoolteacher is the time off, so I figured this would be a great place to visit."

"Then you picked the right place. Wolf here will be the welcome wagon for you in Galveston," she offers her son up like he doesn't clearly work and owns a very successful business.

"It's okay, honestly. I'm sure he's busy." I don't want to put Wolf on the spot. I mean, what if he doesn't feel this crazy ridiculous pull that I do between the two of us?

"Not busy, sunshine. You ready for another one?" he responds, using that same endearment he used earlier before he knew my name.

"Whelp, my job here is done. I made chicken Alfredo with a side of broccoli. There's enough to feed Reese in there too. Don't let him hoard it all. It's made from scratch and one of his favorites. Though, I have a feeling I'll be seeing you around as long as Wolf doesn't screw things up." She gives me a side hug, Wolf a pat to the cheek, and then she's off as fast she came.

"You don't really have to show me around, I promise," I offer him an out now that his mom is gone.

"I have tomorrow off. Well, I have most days off and only come in at night to work in the office while the other bartenders are here. I'll show you the places that tourists don't know about." Wolf takes my empty glass, making me another one without asking or once again taking a payment.

"I'd like that." My voice comes out in a dreamy tone. I swear this man is making me act like a teenager.

"Good, sit here, drink your Sex on the Beach. I'm going to do another check around the bar, then it's my turn to hear everything about you." The huskiness in his tone makes me want to spill my guts to him easily, not that there's much to say, but still, if I'm not careful, I'll tell him more than he'd ever want to hear.

"Okay." This time, I don't suck down my drink as fast as the one earlier. I take my time, enjoying the place and watching Wolf in his element.

THREE

WOLF

IT'S WELL past closing time. Thankfully, it's one of those nights we close at ten o'clock and not at two in the morning like on our busier nights. Sometimes I dread those when we're short staffed and I have to step in to help. Christ, it makes me feel every bit of my thirty-three-year-old self. What shocked me the most tonight was Reese staying the entire time. That could be because we shared the meal my mom brought me, something she does at least twice a week, if not more. Though, Sundays are usually our day to catch up with either dinner out together or at one of our houses.

The only time she attempted to leave was when I did a last call. She dug through her purse, pulled out a few twenty-dollar bills to settle her three-drink tab. "Put your money away. All I ask is when the rest of the folks clear out, you let me spin you around the dance floor." The blush that lit up her cheeks and the coy smile she gave me, it was all I needed. I made sure everything was cleaned up quickly with the servers and customers. Once they were out the door and said doors were locked, that's when my hand went to Reese's, a slow song already playing in the background, and now she's wrapped up in my arms.

"Thank you for tonight." Her head tips up. The few overhead lights I left on when I closed down the bar let me see the richness in her hair, Reese's high cheekbones, the yellow flecks that are interspersed in her green eyes, the long eyelashes that highlight them. But the smile she gives me, it's one I want to see for a very long time. The guy who swore up and down just a few months ago he wasn't ready to settle down, yet here I am holding a woman in my arms and thinking of everything I could see doing with her for the rest of my life, including things like dancing in the kitchen early in the morning or late at night.

"Nothing to thank me for, sunshine. It's me who should be thanking you, staying here your whole night, waiting around on me. I promise I'll make it up to you tomorrow." She settles her head on my chest. My lips graze the top of her head, soaking up the scent of her shampoo, light and airy with a hint of peaches.

"It was fun, and I mean it's not like I was going to do anything else except walk up and down the town until my feet took me back to my cottage." She lifts her head up. I use Reese's hand to spin her around before she's back in my arms again, this time facing out as the beat has picked up a few paces, and we switch to a two-step.

"Just the same. You could have gone back to your place. Which, since you told me you walked here, don't think I'm going to let you walk back by yourself. My truck is out back, or I'll walk you there," I tell her. There isn't a lot of violence out here, more or less party goers who can get rowdy. It's not like I won't be driving back to my place either. It's on the outskirts of Galveston. A ranch-style house on a small patch of land. It may not seem like a whole lot, but it's mine, even if it does need work.

"Whichever is easiest for you will be fine for me." Reese's

head is tipped over her shoulder, my own sinks down, and the softness of her lips meets mine, lightly at first, trying to get a feel to see if this is okay with her or not. When Reese's lips part, I go for broke, devouring her whole, tasting the lingering drink that had me wanting this all damn night. Our tongues tangle. I don't let up, not even when I spin her around in my arms, pick her up by the back of those long-as-hell legs of hers, and carry her to a barstool. My body crowding between her spread thighs, and when she breathes out, "Wolf," I back away from her mouth, fucking reluctantly.

"Sunshine, you make me lose all rational thought," I admit. She plants her forehead in my chest.

"So much the same, but that kiss...it was out of this world amazing." Apparently, we both have no problem telling the other what we're thinking. Fuck, if this is half of what Knox or Trace felt towards their women, no wonder they were dead set on making them theirs.

"It's just the beginning. Let's get you home, sunshine. I think you'll need your beauty rest for tomorrow." I'm not telling her what we're doing yet, wanting to keep it a secret.

"You better, or I might turn into a pumpkin, and that wouldn't be fun for anyone." My hand finds hers as we walk towards the back door. Turning the music and lights off, not letting our hands lose one another the entire time. Yeah, I could really get used to having Reese Miller in my life, permanently.

FOUR
REESE

I'M STILL on cloud nine this morning, coffee in hand, a magazine in the other, and the back porch is calling my name. The kiss Wolf left me with, I swear my lips are still tingling with the last one he gave me when he dropped me off at my place, hands in my hair, his body plastered to mine, and I soaked it all in. My own moans could probably be heard two doors down. Neither of us cared though. We were lost in our own little world, and I can see that continuing to happen. Wolf made sure he had my phone number and I his, then he demanded I lock him out before he took me to bed and I wouldn't see daylight for a few days. I can't say that it would be a bad thing. Clearly, we're not lacking in the chemistry department by any means.

I shake myself out of those thoughts before I have to turn back inside and take out my battery-operated boyfriend like I did last night. It barely took the edge off. My gaze returns to the view of the canal. Birds are chirping, you can hear the water lapping at the sea wall, and the breeze is moving the trees. I'm really glad I picked this spot instead of the more touristy side of the island, not to mention it's so much cheaper too. I plop down on the outdoor couch that's piled with cushions, taking my first sip of the goodness. Coffee made at home just hits differently, it doesn't have all the other crazy stuff most coffee houses make. I just want coffee, sugar, and a splash of flavored creamer. I flip open the magazine, seeing what all is going on in the world of celebrities, not really caring who's the latest and greatest, when my phone chirps from inside the house.

"Ugh, I was just getting comfortable," I grumble but throw my magazine on the couch, not willing to let my cup of coffee go while taking a sip and walking in from the outside. Which is next to impossible when you're as clumsy as I can be.

"Hello," I answer the phone, winded.

"Hey, sunshine, did I catch you at a bad time?" His husky voice comes through on the other end of the line.

"No, my own fault. I didn't think you'd be up this early in the day." I'm an early-bird-gets-the-worm kind of girl. That's not the case with everyone though.

"I've been up with the chickens and cows." The squeal I let out in his ear probably causes him to go deaf.

"I'm seeing I need to schedule a day for you to come over. I even have a few calves right now." For this, I place my coffee down, use my shoulder to hold my phone, and clap like one of the kids in my class who's excited for a new activity.

"Yes, please. Is it possible to do that today? I mean, they're only babies for so long, and it's not like this is something I can see any time of the year where I live." I'm practically inviting myself over, which probably isn't the smartest, but it's baby cows.

"We can do that. I figured you'd want to see some of Galveston, but if farm animals are what you're after, I'll come pick you up shortly," he offers.

"I'd love that. Would you rather I drive to you instead? It doesn't make much sense having you drive all the way over here to turn around and drive back too." Even though we just met last night, the hours we've spent together have made it feel like Wolf and I have known each other for months instead.

"Not a problem, sunshine. I have to stop at the bar and bank, then I'll swing by your place to pick you up. Will you be ready in an hour or so?" he asks.

"I can be ready in less than thirty minutes if need be." I'm already heading towards the master bedroom. What was once going to be a lazy morning is definitely turning into a hurry up and start the day instead.

"No rush, I'll call you when I'm about ten minutes out." I'm not even sure if I have clothes to wear to someplace that has animals. I mean when I packed, it was for the beach. This might be harder than I thought.

"That's fine. I still need to eat and figure out first world problems in the form of clothing." A laugh bubbles out of me. I hear his deep chuckle on the other end, making my heart beat faster because Wolf is seemingly taking me like I am.

"It's not that hard, sunshine. Throw on a shirt, some shorts, and closed toed shoes. If you're wanting to hang with the animals, you don't want to step in manure." I really should have packed better.

"That might be a problem. All I have is a pair of slip-on shoes. Will that be okay?" I ask, if anything, I can run to the store, buy some cheap shoes, and go from there.

"Should be. If not, I know Mom leaves shoes here all the time when she's out at the house to grab eggs from the hens or when I need her to meet the neighbor to come get his heifers out of my pasture and I'm at work." I guess that solves my shoe problem.

"That works. I'll be ready whenever you are. Thank you, Wolf." A dreamy sigh escapes my lips.

"Sunshine, it's really not a lot. You're welcome though.

Now, go eat something and get ready. Hopefully, this doesn't take longer than normal, and I'll be your way soon enough," Wolf responds.

"Alright, see you soon." My mind is already in a whirlwind of what could happen. One thing's for sure, all of my worries have seemed to disappear since the moment my eyes landed on Wolf. A job that's slowly drowning out my joy is a distant memory, and for that I'm thankful.

"Later, Reese." We hang up, my mind goes to food and once again my clothing choice. I don't want Wolf to have to wait around on me. Plus, I can't wait to see Wolf in his surroundings.

FIVE
WOLF

REESE IS WHOLEHEARTEDLY into being on my small farm. It's only five acres, nothing like what my friends have in their backyards. This works for me though, it's enough to make some extra money, and it's what I do in my downtime, a way to decompress. With Reese here, though, it's like I'm experiencing all of her firsts vicariously through her. The smile that's been plastered on her face the past hour is enough for me to stand outside here all day, even when she's wearing my mom's mud boots that are two sizes too big.

"You're enjoying this, aren't you?" She's sitting in the field, grass surrounding her, waiting to see if one of the baby calves will leave its mother's side so she can pet it.

"Yep, I sure am."

"I'm thinking you might have to wait another week or so. Then the cows might come closer." I hop over the fence that I was leaning on instead of using the gate. The way Reese bites at her lower lip, telling me she enjoyed the view, has me strutting like a peacock towards her.

"Then I'll have to come back." I sit down behind her,

spreading my legs around hers, allowing her to lean back, giving me her weight. To be fair, the need to have her surrounding me or touching her has fast become an obsession.

"Anytime you want to come out here, you're more than welcome to." My place is only a thirty-minute commute from Galveston, where the bar is, but the place I call home is definitely here in Hitchcock. Whereas Mom lives in the height of the beach area, I chose to find something that would suit my needs and had some type of farmland, like I did as a child.

"You better watch out. I might overstay my welcome." Reese's head moves to my shoulder. A purr leaves her lips when I tip my head down, lightly grazing my lips against the column of her neck.

"I'm thinking that won't happen, sunshine." The nickname matches the way she lights up a dark and gloomy room with her smile.

"Don't be too sure of yourself." My lips find hers, shutting her up in the best way possible while I get the joy of tasting her again. A growl leaves my throat as my hands glide a path from her stomach to beneath her thin tank top, moving it along her smooth skin. Her stomach flexes, back arching to get me where she wants my hands the most. My girl, she's definitely greedy. The tips of my fingers pull down the cups of her bra, her tank top is bunched at the top, and the view I have of her... Fuck, it's going to make me come undone.

"Please," Reese breathes against my lips. One hand cups her breast, my fingers rolling her cherry-color-tipped nipple. The way her hips are undulating, I know what I'm doing next.

"You want my fingers inside you, sunshine?" I break apart from our kiss, needing to see the desire in her eyes.

"I shouldn't, it's too soon, but yes, so much yes." She starts to move her body, but there's no way I'm letting that happen. Reese is staying right where she is.

"Don't move." Her body freeze in its place, lips plump from our kiss, sun beating down on her bare skin, and this time, she watches as my other hand glides down the center of her stomach. Thank God she's wearing a pair of stretchy shorts. There are no buttons to hinder where I'm dying to be. My hand moves over the fabric of her panties, wanting to tease her until she's on the edge and will tip over with one thrust of my fingers.

"Fuck, that's sexy," I grunt when I feel just how wet she is. She's saturated, soaked through. Damn, our kisses and teasing her lightly has set her on fire. I can only imagine what she'll get like once my cock is buried deep inside her.

"More." One of her hands moves on top of mine. I slide her panties to the side and am met with smooth and silky skin, wetness coating my fingers.

"What I wouldn't do to have your flavor on my lips." I know she can feel my thick and heavy cock against her ass with the way she's wiggling it against me.

"Yes." Reese's throaty murmur has me sliding one finger inside her, seeing how much she can take. The gripping of her cunt is enough to make me want to tear our clothes off and fuck my seed deep inside her womb.

"So fucking tight. You're going to destroy me, sunshine." My lips lock on hers, swallowing down her moans. I slide another finger inside of her, wanting her to get used to what it will feel like to be stuffed full of me, that it won't hurt her.

"Wolf." Reese's body shakes beneath my ministrations, with her hand on top of mine, showing me what she likes, and it's a hell of a show.

"You going to come for me, sunshine?" I ask. Her eyes lock on mine. I scissor my fingers inside her while using the palm of my hand on her clit.

"Yes." Her eyes close, her cunt clamps down on my fingers, and a gush of wetness coats me, making me want inside her even more. Reese's body collapses against me after she orgasms. I keep my fingers inside her, not wanting to leave her body just yet.

"Fuck, I know once I get inside you, sunshine, I won't ever leave," I admit. Her eyes open. She's got a dreamy look on her face, and my heart practically beats out of its chest with the knowledge that I did that to her.

SIX
REESE

I WATCH as Wolf pulls his fingers out of my center. He doesn't wipe them off, instead, he licks his fingers, humming in satisfaction. It causes my core to clench with need again. Clearly, my body is a hussy.

"Sunshine, you taste so fucking good." That's it. There's no way I will be able to sit here any longer. I want to return the favor in the worst possible way. It's probably why I hurriedly climb up on my knees, hands going to his chest, and push him until his back is on the ground.

"You wanting something, sunshine?" Wolf asks, fingers delving in my hair as my face hovers over his.

"Yes, I want to taste you, put my mouth on you." I'm whispering for no reason, the only things out here are the animals, the trees, and a breeze.

"You don't have to. It's not a tit-for-tat kind of deal." This man, he's going to rock my world.

"I know that, but I want to." He does an ab curl, sitting up with me straddling his lap this time. My hands slide from his chest, lifting his shirt along the way.

"Off." He chuckles but does that thing it seems only men can do, taking it off one handed by the back of the neck. Tan skin appears before my eyes, muscles flexing, and my mouth salivates, but Wolf has other ideas as his lips seek mine out, our tongues meeting, both of us tasting one another. It gives me the time to move my hands down the length of his chest, my nails sinking into his muscles along the way.

"You unbutton my pants, sunshine, there's no turning back. You hear me?" Wolf grabs my hands as they move to the denim at his waist.

"I know that I'm prepared for it. Are you?" I arch my eyebrows, obsidian blue eyes meeting my green ones.

"I'm all fucking in." He nods his head, then my hands fumble with his button until I get the hang of it. Wolf has the patience of a saint until I finally open the fly of his pants. Skin meets skin. He clearly isn't a fan of boxers or any other kind of underwear, and I'm reaping the benefits of it now. He lifts me up as I push his pants down. "Holy shit," whooshes out of me as my hand wraps around his length. My fingers don't even touch. Wolf must be as wide as my damn wrist, not really, but oh my gosh his girth, not to mention his length. It's standing up proudly, going up to his navel, and I'm worried there's no way he'll ever fit inside me.

"Now you know why I wanted to ease you into this." He groans as I use my fist, my thumb sweeping over the tip, gathering his pre-cum before sliding it down along his length.

"Are you sure that's going to fit inside me?" I mumble, but my eyes aren't on his, they're firmly planted on the way his cock looks wrapped inside my hand, smooth velvet, causing me to moisten my lips.

"It'll fit. Might take time, but you'll be molded to me soon enough, sunshine." Wolf grasps my hips, not letting me move. I'm apparently not using my mouth today, which might be a good thing because lockjaw could potentially happen. Instead, I bring down my other hand, wrapping it around the top so they're stacked on top of one another.

"Reese." The way my name rushes out of Wolf, deep in timbre with that husky tone, I double up my efforts, watching for every little nuance that he likes what I'm doing, using it to my advantage. His hips move up every time my hands sink down.

"God, now I know how you felt watching me," I mutter. Wolf's hands travel up to my hair, sink into the loose waves.

"You have no idea what you're doing to me, sunshine. You're killing me bit by bit in the best way imaginable." Wolf brings his lips to mine, his body locks up beneath me, and I feel his hot cum jet onto my hands. He doesn't stop coming even after he breaks the kiss while groaning. My eyes take it all in. It's got to be the sexiest thing in this world, and I'm the one who did this to him and for him.

"Yep, we're going to have to do that again, and soon." My breasts meet his chest, bra still bunched beneath them, my shirt still on top. I probably look like a hot mess. But the way Wolf has me pressed against him, he clearly doesn't mind how I look or the mess we've made on one another.

"Yeah, as soon as I catch my breath. Next time, I'm using my mouth though." And I swear with his words alone, I just had another orgasm. "My woman likes that idea, huh?" Wolf asks, clearly feeling what my body is giving off.

"God, yes," I reply. The next thing I know, I'm up and in Wolf's arms and he's carrying me through the pasture and up to his ranch. I guess he intends to make good on his promise.

SEVEN
WOLF

MY PLANS of taking Reese to bed were derailed when her stomach rumbled, so instead, I dropped her off in my bathroom. It was hard not to stay in there and watch the water sluice off Reese's curvy body. The fact that she wasn't worried about the mess on her body or her hands, and just went with the flow, it hit me square in the chest, this woman allowing me to mark her like Tarzan would, not even batting an eye. If I stayed, though, and washed our bodies together, we'd be doing a whole lot more, but there was no way I'd allow her to starve. Even if my baser needs are what is starving right now.

I walked away with her tits out ripe for my mouth, the shower running, and me placing a shirt on the counter, one of mine that has the bar's logo emblazoned across the front of it. Nothing better than my name on her. Shit, if I had it my way, I'd have Reese wear it everywhere so the whole world would know she's mine. I grabbed her a pair of boxers I'm forced to wear if I need to dress up. Thankfully, those times are few and far between. As for me, I relegated myself to the downstairs bathroom. If it weren't for my cock and stomach coated with my cum, I wouldn't even need a shower. It didn't take me long, a quick wash and rinse, then I'm in the kitchen after changing into a new set of clothes. This time a pair of grey sweatpants and black shirt. With it getting later on in the afternoon, I'm not seeing the need to get back into jeans until it's time to get to the bar.

I'm putting together a couple of sandwiches—ham, turkey, cheese, mayo, mustard, with thin slices of tomato and lettuce—when Reese clears her throat. "I wasn't sure where you wanted my towel, so I hung it on the back of the door." She places her clothes on top of her purse, giving me a glimpse of her panties. Fuck, knowing she's bare beneath the borrowed shorts is doing nothing for my re-hardening cock.

"That's fine." I lick my lower lip as she walks towards me, a sway in her hips that Reese is completely unaware of.

"Can I help with anything?"

"Sure, you want to grab a couple of drinks? There's some fruit in the fridge, and chips in the pantry." I may live on my own, but that doesn't mean my house looks like a cold, stark place or that I have no food. My mom may think otherwise with the way she brings food to the bar, but it's more for her sake than mine. After so many years of it just being the two of us, she doesn't know how to cook food for just one person, not that I can blame her. It's damn hard, and you always seem to have a shit ton of leftovers.

"Your place is amazing, really. The land, the animals, the house, it's everything." Reese has told me she rents an apartment in the same district where she teaches. It's costing her a mint, and everyone knows when you're a teacher, you don't get paid very much. Even when you work at a prestigious private school.

"Thank you. I was serious when I told you you're welcome here anytime. In fact, I was going to see if you wanted to stay here tonight. I'm not going to be gone that long. I'd love nothing more than to come back here and you be here." Reese may say no. She is renting a condo on the intracoastal this summer. I'm hoping she'll say yes though.

"That shouldn't be a problem, as long as you have an extra toothbrush." I plate the rest of the sandwiches, almost dropping them when she gives in so sweetly.

"Fuck, yes. Me coming home to you in my bed, it must be my lucky fucking day." I stop what I'm doing, wipe my hands off with a towel, and then I'm on Reese in a flash, lips meeting hers lightly. Clearly, taking things slow with her isn't an option, not with this soul-consuming need.

"Maybe we can go back and forth, but stay here more because you have animals. I hate to pay for a place I'm not staying at either though," Reese says when we pull a part.

"We can do that, or you can cancel your vacation and just stay here." I may as well go for broke while I'm at it.

"That's something to think about. Can we do it the other way for a little bit?" Her eyes are full of hope, and I'd never dream of dimming them.

"Anything you want, sunshine. Anything at all." I squeeze her hip, smile at her. It's the damn truth. I don't give a fuck that we just met. When you meet that one person who lifts a heaviness off your shoulders you didn't know you're carrying, you know it's the real deal, the whole damn enchilada.

"Thank you." I'm not sure if she's talking about compromising or the meal. Either way, I nod at her as we sit down at the eat-in kitchen table and tuck into our food.

EIGHT
REESE

WE SPENT the rest of the day until Wolf had to go to work relaxing, learning so many things about one another. Like when how his dad passed away when he was only six years old, his mother never felt the need to bring another man into either of their lives. He said it wasn't always easy, nonetheless, he was thankful he had his friend's dad to pick up the pieces. Little did I know that my man can apparently ride a bucking bronc like nobody's business. I mean sure, Mrs. Shaw touched on how he squirreled all of his money away, but she didn't really go into detail that as soon as he graduated high school, he was hell bent on making it. Which he did, to nationals, twice, then he stopped before it got to his head. He came back home, helped pay off his mom's house. She apparently cussed him out and ran after him with a flip flop, threatening to whoop his tail. That part had me snickering. She seemed so sweet the one time I met her that I can't imagine any of that happening. I told Wolf how miserable I am at my job, how uptight all the faculty is and how opinions are like assholes in the school, in which everyone has one. He suggested that if I'm that unhappy, maybe finding a new school to work at would be better, and then I wouldn't feel so burnt out. Wolf isn't wrong in that aspect. It's still scary though.

When he left for work, my lips felt the aftermath along with the aching between my legs. I did what any woman would do—I looked at every nook and cranny I could. It turned up nothing, thankfully. Wolf's home may be on the older side, like much older, it's probably in the historic category. It's been remodeled somewhat, like the kitchen and living room in the downstairs area. The master bedroom and bathroom were done. It's kept with the time period too, with its gleaming hardwood floors, soft paint colors, furniture that's built for comfort and made of real leather. What had me stopping in my tracks was the back of the house. It's been untouched, but I could imagine so many things happening with it. If it were screened in, it could be used well beyond the summer months, and even into winter if you had some of those portable propane heaters. A daybed swing, draped with pillows and blankets, where you could relax while enjoying an evening snuggled up together. It would be perfect, the cows mooing in the distance along with the noises of the chickens. I wonder if this goes where I'm pretty sure it is going if he'd let me add some pigs and donkeys to the mix.

I'm nestled in the pillows and blankets of Wolf's bed. I tried to hold out as long as I could, but once it hit eleven o'clock at night, my eyes started drooping. And, let's face it, there's only so much snooping a girl can do. There were a few photos with friends at a rodeo, all of them standing together, Wolf in the middle. The guys on each side of him were clearly brothers. I left the television on when I moved my way up here to help with the stillness of the night. It's how I've always slept, the quiet making my mind work non-stop if not. That must be why I didn't hear Wolf come in.

"Hmm," I mumble when a hand glides over my stomach while another travels under the nape of my neck. The fresh scent of Wolf's soap I used earlier today, an earthy scent, reminding me of fresh air with an undertone of leather.

"Shhh, sleep, sunshine," Wolf murmurs in my ear, giving my body the opposite effect of falling back asleep, not with the way his rasp causes goose bumps to pebble along the skin of my body.

"Wolf." I took off his boxer briefs before sliding into his bed. I never wear panties to bed, and maybe, just maybe, I was thinking something else would happen too. Which seems to be the case now because my shirt is rucked up from the shifting of my body while sleeping and I can feel Wolf's bare cock notch between the globes of my ass.

"Fuck," I hear him grumble, but instead of doing anything about both of us being bare to each other, he glides his hand up the length of my torso until the palm of his hand is full of my breast. Sleeping is going to be damn near impossible with the way he's perfectly aligned to my body.

"God." The way he's pulling at my nipple, it's making me want to turn around and literally attack him.

"Not tonight. You want me in the morning, I'm yours. For now, you sleep." I guess that's putting a damper on things, which sucks, but Wolf is probably right. I look at the alarm clock he keeps on the nightstand and see that it's well after three o'clock in the morning. Wolf must be exhausted. So much for him not being gone long. Things must have been busy at the bar, or he ran into trouble.

"Okay, you win. This time at least." It doesn't stop me from wiggling my ass or for Wolf to push into me from behind. God, how easy it would be for him to slide inside me, even with the girth slightly worrying me. I bet the pain would be worth it for the pleasure.

"Get some sleep, sunshine. I know you'll be raring to go the minute the sun peaks over the horizon." He kisses me beneath my ear, and I swear he does it on purpose.

"Good night," I respond.

"Night, sunshine." His voice, it's so deep and sultry that I could listen to him talk forever. My eyes close, and I cherish the feeling of him surrounding me.

NINE
WOLF

SLEEPING with Reese is not easy. I'm not sure if she realizes how much the squirming did to my hard-on. At one point, her hand was on my cock, not jacking it off, just holding it, like she was making sure I wasn't going anywhere. I wouldn't leave her, not even if the fires of hell were after me.

Now, Reese's head is in the crook of my neck, leg hiked up and over my hip. Her warm center just hovering over my cock. I know one slight movement and I could be inside her. Not to mention she somehow lost her shirt in the midst of her moving around. I'll have to make a note of just stripping her down naked before getting into bed at night. That and turning the air down, something I forgot to do last night, between my body heat and her twisting and turning.

"Wolf." I guess my woman is awake judging by the way she's licking the slope of my neck before nibbling on it. My body moves just the right way so the head of cock notches at the entrance to her pussy.

"Please be awake, Reese," I groan, wanting her to be a willing participant the first time I slide inside her. The next time, I won't mind fucking her until she wakes up, but this time, I want her eyes wide open.

"I'm awake. Stop dilly-dallying and fuck me already." Demanding little thing she is this morning.

"You asked for it." I move her body until she's practically on top of me, while I'm somewhat on my side. My eyes move to hers and then down where the lips of her pussy are flared on each side of my cock.

"Go slow. You're so big." One of her hands reaches my shoulder, the other attempting to sneak down to her clit.

"No, you don't, sunshine. You're coming with my cock inside your cunt, not with your fingers." I smack her hand away. Her head sinks back, baring the column of her throat, her pretty tits heaving with the way Reese's body shakes as I give her another inch of my cock.

"God." Her moan resonates deep inside me, and as desperately as I want to sink inside her with one forward thrust, I don't want to hurt her.

"You ready for more?" I grunt while taking a deep breath. Sweat is coating both of our bodies, each of us needing something more to latch onto.

"If you don't, I'm going to take over myself," Reese smarts off. I do something completely opposite of what she wants—I dip my head, taking one of her pretty nipples into my mouth. I use my teeth, and she arches into me, accepting my cock another inch inside her.

"You ready? I'm going to slide home," I groan. Reese's cunt is fluttering around me, causing my balls to tighten.

"Yes." She quivers in my arms. My body flips her onto her back, giving me traction to thrust into her wet heat.

"Fuck, sunshine. It's like you're sucking my body into yours," I stutter into the thrusting of my hips.

"You feel so good," she responds. Shit, the way Reese

always responds to me, it's enough to make me come. I hold off, barely.

"I need your mouth, Wolf. I want my lips on yours." Her greedy hands grip my shoulders, pressing into them so firmly I bet by tomorrow, I'll have bruises from her nails. That thought only eggs me on, wanting to see just how bad the marks she'll leave can get. I bend down, teasing her lips with mine, gently grazing ours together. Reese loves the buildup, I could see that from yesterday alone.

"You're mine, sunshine. This solidifies it. No running, no leaving, you're tied to me, and I'm tied to you." The sigh she lets out, my woman, she gets it.

"I'm not going anywhere, Wolf. I promise." At the conviction in Reese's tone, I work her body harder, my own responding to hers. I bring my thumb to her bundle of nerves, wanting her to light up like a firecracker on a hot July night.

"Get there, sunshine. Grip my cock so tight, you make me come," I demand. My hips don't stop moving, and every time I'm completely inside her, I swivel my hips. I watch as Reese's eyes close, head arching back into the pillows, body bowing tightly, her cunt clenching my cock, I can't hold back anymore. My cum jets inside of Reese, painting the walls of her pussy, my eyes moving to where we're joined, seeing the mix of us together. At this rate, my cock will never go down. Not with the memories we keep making.

"Wolf, it's so intense." Sweetness is dripping off her I mash my lips to hers, body replete, and it's hard not to fuck her again and again.

"I feel it too, sunshine. It's only going to get better," I murmur in her ear.

"If it gets any better, I may combust." She laughs, causing me to let out a chuckle of my own out.

"Not gonna complain. You want to lie like this for a minute

or clean up?" I ask as I bring her on top of me, not giving a damn that we'll be making a complete mess of the sheets.

"Like this, please." Her head rests on my chest while my fingers glide along her spine, both of us content in the best way possible, even if my cock is ready to go again. That won't be happening, not until I see how she feels. I'm not going to hurt her just because I can't control my dick when she's around. The thought of taking care of Reese, though, that's something I'll definitely enjoy doing.

TEN
REESE

WE'VE SETTLED into this way of life for the past few days, alternating between my place and Wolf's. I didn't see it coming that I'd be more comfortable at his place than the one I rented for the summer. Wolf hasn't pushed or pressured me into giving up my rental, but I did look at the contract I signed for the summer, and let's just say there's a clause that I can do an early out. I'd be out of a deposit, but with the way I'm spending gas left and right while commuting back and forth, it'd be worth it.

That's why I'm trying to figure out how to bring it up to Wolf without looking like a total dork. The other thing on my agenda today is buying some boots. His mom's have done in a pinch, but it takes twice the time to get out and help in the morning or evenings, and let's just say, you do not want to fall in cow shit. I've done it twice now. Both times have had me laughing my ass off and one time, Wolf even threw me in the stock tank to rinse me off after I fell flat on my back. I pulled Wolf down with me. It might have started out as fun, but it definitely got hot and heavy really quick.

"Hi, Mrs. Julia." I wave when I see Wolf's mom. She offered to meet me at the local western wear place.

"Hey there, Reese. You ready to shop the day away?" she asks, hugging me close to her like I'm an extension of her.

"I sure am, though your son warned me that I may come home exhausted and broke," I joke with her. Wolf's mom is a hoot. I got a text last night telling me who it was and what we we're doing today. Wolf said to not even attempt getting out of it because she'd just find out where I was and drag me along no matter what. It didn't bother me. I had things to get anyway.

"That boy, he's all talk. I won't wear you out too much. Whose place are you staying at tonight?" Wolf told me they were close, and apparently, they really are. I'd like to say that I'm close to my mom, but I'm not sure that we're this close. Though, I did tell her and Daddy about Wolf, how we've spent time together, and that I really like him. My mom said to have fun. Daddy was ready to do a background check, which I'm sure he's already done. When I moved to the area where I work now, it took me an hour away from my family. It's caused us not to see each other like we used to, though once a month, I try to make sure I go visit them or they come down to see me. I need to make sure they get down here for at least a weekend before I turn the rental back over to its owners. They may as well have some fun too, that is if Momma can get Daddy away from the house. He doesn't like to venture far even though they're both retired now.

"I'm not sure. I think at Wolf's. I hate to leave the animals and then him getting up early after being at the bar. At least if I'm there, I can sneak out of bed, feed the animals while he's sleeping, and when he wakes up, fix us something to eat before we head out to sightsee." Yesterday, we went to the moody gardens. That was so much fun. We've even seen some historical areas, which really had me smiling. I'm a sucker for history, and the area is entrenched with it.

"That's great to hear. you both know if you stay on the island, I have no problem feeding the animals, right?"

"Yes, but what sense does that make for you? Wolf mentioned me just staying with him and letting my rental go for the summer. I'm seriously contemplating it. Of course, I'd still pay for staying with him. Us staying on the island even when he's not working is silly. Plus, we've seen just about every mile of Galveston in the past two days." Which has been fun, but Wolf is seriously holding out in the sex department lately. He'll give me his mouth, and I'll return the favor, but other than that it's been zilch. And I'm getting really tired of him using the excuse that I need to heal. Yes, he's bigger, like ridiculously so, but I'm not going to die from big-cock-itis either.

"You can't argue with logistics. The two of you remind me of myself when I met Wolf's dad. God bless his soul, he was a great man and taken from us too soon, but Bobby would have loved you and Wolf together. We knew right away that we were meant to be together, got married on our third date, had Wolf a year or so later, and when he left this earth, my heart left with him." My heart absolutely aches for her. Tears are in both of our eyes. I do the only thing I can. No words can help ease that, and even now, twenty-plus years later, she still feels so deeply for him. Wolf told me how he lost his dad to a drunk driver when he was six years old. It was a pretty big blow to the whole town from what he said. Everyone knew everyone. It happened and one night when he was coming back from a cattle auction. Wolf woke up to the devastating news. I can't even imagine how much their life has changed since then.

I hug her, the woman who raised an amazingly strong son who I'm relentlessly falling in love with shared her story with me, and now we're both a blubbering mess in the middle of a parking lot.

"Oh gosh, I'm so sorry. Talking about Bobby, it still gets to me. Wolf didn't understand for the longest time why I refused to date or move on. I'm willing to bet he does now." We part from our hug. Mrs. Julia is waving her hands at her face, trying to dry her tears, while I'm using the back of my hand on mine.

"Don't apologize ever. To have a love like that, it has to be the greatest of all time." I'm sure she's right when it comes to Wolf and me. The bond and connection we've formed already, there's no way our hearts can deny it.

"Oh, anyway. Let's go see what kind of damage we can do." She pulls herself together, struts inside the store like she was made to take control. What did I tell you, that woman is so damn strong. I only hope that I'll be half as strong as she is if I ever have to go through something like that.

ELEVEN
WOLF

"WELL, look what the cat dragged in," I tell Creed, a friend I've known for a couple of years now. He only comes in when he's passing through, a lineman by trade, but on his down time you can find him at a rodeo. The man has balls of steel to get on a broncing buck at his age. At the age of thirty-two, there is no way in hell you'd see me doing that. Fucking crazy is what he is.

"Hey, man." I walk towards him, shaking his hand and pulling him in for a one-armed hug. "Yeah. Figured I'd stop by before I get back home. Taking a job working locally from now on. You'll probably see less of me unless you actually get out of this place more."

"Who says I don't get away from the island? If you were home more, you'd see that I was at my place a fuck of a lot more lately." I'm home more than ever now, and the bar isn't suffering from it either.

"No shit? Well, then, maybe I'll see you more." I walk back around to the bar while he takes a seat on an empty stool.

"Yep, that will happen when you find a woman like Reese." His eyes perk up.

"You found someone who's got you settling down? Congrats, man." I hand him a bottle of Coors, popping the cap open.

"She's one of a kind. What has you working locally now? Getting tired of traveling so much?" I ask. It'll be nice as hell to have him back home.

"Rhett's sister, Laney, called me. Apparently, their dad is retired, reluctantly, but it left them in a bind. Leaving Rhett to do a majority of the work. Laney was bawling her eyes out. So, here I am, but if you're home more, I'm sure I'll see you around." Creed, Rhett, and I live in the same area, Rhett's family owning a bigger spread than Creed and me.

"Laney called you, huh?" I poke the bear, knowing full well there was a reason he went to work traveling the entire fucking state, leaving his own small ranch and hiring a hand to take care of his livestock.

"Don't start. I'm not coming back for her. Only trying to be neighborly and lend a helping hand." Creed is so full of shit, but now isn't the time to give him shit, not with the way he's looking like the weight of the world is on his shoulders.

"Let me know if I can help. Reese and I are home more often than not. I'm pretty sure she'll be here permanently once summer is over," I offer.

"I appreciate that. Might help Laney to have a friend around too." That I can attest to. I might even see if my mom would be interested in doing a girl's day with Reese too. I know today she and Reese are out shopping, which if I know my mom, they'll both come back exhausted and with a car full of bags.

"No problem." We shoot the shit for a little bit. He tells me some of the stories of the crazy people who were cussing a blue streak when their power wasn't turned on right away or if they were transferring lines over. I don't know how he kept his cool while doing such a dangerous job, and in the heat at that. Creed is the type of person to let shit slide down his back, not tackling anything, until he's at his limit, then all hell breaks loose, and I have a feeling once he's home for a few days, we'll all be in for one hell of a surprise, including Rhett.

TWELVE

REESE

"OH MY GOD, you weren't kidding about my feet falling off when it comes to shopping with your mom," I bemoan overly dramatic. Wolf wasn't home when my car finally pulled itself into the driveway. Okay, it didn't do that on its own, but with how exhausted I was, my body was on autopilot the entire drive here. And I still had to unload my car. There was plenty too—clothes, boots, a few things for around Wolf's house. Which could be a good thing or a bad thing, depending on how he takes what I've added to not only inside of the house but also on his front porch.

"I warned you. Come here, sunshine." I'm standing in the kitchen, dicing up tomatoes to go with a fast dinner of oven fried chimichangas. The way his voice comes out, deep and grumbly, I stop what I'm doing, my feet ready and willing to go anywhere with him. Which is why when I bought things for his place, it wasn't just for him. It was for me too.

"Hey." My voice cracks. Wolf's hands move to my hips, his lips meet mine, lightly grazing them, and then he's pulling me in for a hug. Apparently, he's not upset about the new cushions

I bought for the outdoor swing or the plethora of pots, though I'll need his help with the use of his truck to go to the nursery.

"Sunshine, need you to know here and now, I'm not letting you leave me. In fact, before your parents get here next week, you may just want them to pack your place." I pull back from him, secretly whooping it up in happiness inside my soul but also trying not to bust a gut laughing.

"As amazing as that sounds, you clearly haven't met my parents yet. They love me like the dickens, but they'd never pack my house for me. Plus, Mom and Dad will definitely have you answering to their twenty-one questions, rapid fire like." I let out a laugh because Wolf has no idea what he's in for.

"Pretty sure I can deal with that. You and I can go bring everything down here after they meet me." He's got it all planned out, and while I love that about him, I still have one issue.

"Um, not to ruin your fun, but there is this little thing I need to think about. Okay, maybe two things. My apartment lease, which if I break it, I'm out some money. That's not too much of an issue, but the other, it's a big contender," I tell him. Wolf still hasn't said anything about all the changes I've made, so I'm kind of wondering if he's that kind of male, much like my own father, who doesn't notice anything.

"What's that?" His hands rest on his hips. I roll my eyes at this alpha stance he's taking.

"A j-o-b," I spell out. There's no way in hell I'll ever live off someone for free or not have some kind of steady income. "Don't, do not even say what I'm pretty sure I know you'll be saying. I get that you want to take care of me, and I'm wholly grateful for it, but a woman has to be able to stand on her own two feet too."

"Well, you know damn well that I will, and I have plenty of it to go around. I didn't scrimp, scour, and save for nothing. I understand where you're coming from, but it's not like there aren't schools in this area. You even said so yourself that you're wanting a change. No one says you can't take a break to see what's around Hitchcock or the surrounding areas. Though, you may not make as much money as you did before." I walk away when Wolf starts talking about me quitting my job, not wanting to blow this out of proportion. I know what he's trying to do, and I know he's coming from a good place, but I'm not sure my independent streak will allow me to even fathom his offer.

"This place is yours though, Wolf. It's not mine. I didn't help you with it and you pay for everything. I can't even buy groceries without you feeling the need to reimburse me." The chopping of my tomatoes echoes through the kitchen, probably with more vigor than necessary.

"Put the knife down, Reese." Wolf is prowling towards me when I stop what I'm doing. My eyes take him in—black shirt, dark blue jeans, and boots. His standard workwear, but the heat in his eyes, the conviction behind those words, it's hard not to listen to him.

"I don't want to fight, Wolf." I really don't. I hate confrontation like nobody's business.

"Not going to fight, sunshine. I'm going to convince you in every way imaginable to have faith in not only me, but in us." Wolf bends at the waist, hoisting me up and over his shoulder. One arm bands around my legs, the other smacking my ass. I guess this is Wolf's way of making up, though I think I'll be the one reaping all the benefits.

THIRTEEN
WOLF

THIS IS GOING to fucking suck, massively. I've had Reese in my bed or me in hers at the rental house for the entire time since we've met. Now her parents are here in Galveston, and she'll be staying with them while they're here. I get it. For Christ's sake, it was my idea. Reese let me know just how much of a stickler her dad was and that he was set in his ways. I imagine if I had a daughter like Reese, I'd be the exact same way. Fuck, I may be even worse than Mr. Miller.

It still doesn't make it any easier lying in bed tonight alone, thinking about last night, Reese in this very bed, legs spread wide, bare cunt on display, chest heaving from the way I kissed the slope of her neck, nipping and teasing along the way until my face was hovering over Reese's center. All the begging and pleading she did, my ears heard it, but there was no way I would rush through the process of tasting her. I can still hear her moaning as my tongue traced the lips of her pussy, humming my happiness at the way Reese's legs clamped down on my head, trapping me.

"Christ," I groan. These thoughts are going to do nothing

but make me having to use my fist instead of the velvet heat of Reese. She was dripping so much of her sweetness when my tongue finally fucked her that Reese came instantly. I didn't let up though, I kept going further, my thumb finding her back entrance, pressing on it lightly. Allowing Reese to get the feel of it, but I kid you not, she opened up around me, ground her whole body on me and let my thumb push inside with the help of her cum. Fuck, when she came for the second time, it was with my tongue in her cunt, like my cock desperately wanted to be, my thumb being clenched by her ass, and her hands grasping at the strands of my hair while she did a full-body shiver.

I launch myself out of my bed, heading to the back door, knowing that I won't be getting any sleep tonight and may as well be productive. If it weren't for the fact that we're all meeting for breakfast tomorrow, I'd have gone to the bar tonight to work on the orders, schedules, and books. Instead, I'm home alone in this big empty house, something I never noticed when I first bought it, but now that Reese has been here, filling it with her laughter, little touches around the house, and her presence, it's as silent as tomb, fucking awful. Even the cows and chickens aren't happy that she's not home. Reese is known for feeding them first thing in the morning, allowing me to sleep in if I've worked late at the bar. She'll come outside, give them food, clean water, even work on the hen house all while talking to them like they're her children in a classroom. Don't even get me started on hearing Reese talk about adding more animals to the bunch, which is why I'm on my way out to the barn. I heard her saying to the animals we should add pigs and donkeys into the mix, but I'm drawing the line at pigs. I don't mind donkeys, but a pig is a whole other story. Those wily things love to rut in the ground and can become escape artists too. That's the reason I'm at the barn, checking in on the newest addition. A young brown and tan donkey is now residing in there, alone.

"I hope I didn't fuck up," I grumble as I step into my boots, then make my way to where the little fella is staying. I'm thinking about him out there by himself. The chickens are in their area, the cows grazing the fields, so he's on his own. If he doesn't do okay on his own, I might need to see if we can find another one for him to hang out with. I've clearly been hanging out with Reese too much because before her I wouldn't have even had these thoughts. Now that she's a part of my life though, she's settled deep in my heart and soul. It's causing me to take a look at everything, in the best way possible.

My eyes must be deceiving me because when I walk into the barn, there's the donkey I bought for Reese curled up in the corner, but there's also the woman I've been missing more than ever, tucked in beside him.

FOURTEEN
REESE

I PROBABLY SHOULD HAVE PEELED my eyes open the minute Wolf wrapped me up in his arms. I knew it was him by his scent alone—in a crowded room, blindfolded, my body would gravitate towards Wolf. But I didn't because after the full-blown argument I had with my father over the fact that I'm completely and helplessly in love with the man who's carrying me inside his home, I'm slap worn out and so disappointed in how it was handled that I'm completely wrung out. And let's just say the shit hit the fan. I grabbed my purse, keys, and ran to him. I was silent as a mouse when pulling up to his house, going so far as cutting off my headlights, not slamming my door, and not jangling my keys. That stopped when I heard a new sound coming from the barn, almost as if an animal was crooning out towards the night air. The moment my eyes locked on the donkey that must be a little over a year old, my feet took me towards him. I prayed that Wolf didn't name him, because my mind was already made up when it came to what he should be called. Dominic was beyond fitting for him, and when he nudged my hand, begging to be petted, that's what I did.

"Wolf." I breathe him in, my nose in the crook of his neck.

"Not that I don't mind having you in my arms, sunshine. But what are you doing home and in the barn with your surprise?" My eyes pop open.

"You brought Dominic home for me?" I don't touch on the first question yet.

"Yeah, it was supposed to be for when you came over tomorrow afternoon after we have breakfast with your parents. You care to answer my question?" I motion for him to let me down, dreading this talk because this could very well ruin our plans for tomorrow morning and doing the whole schmoozing thing.

"About that, let's just say Dad isn't willing to budge on meeting you tomorrow, and he's basically said he'll cut me off if I move down here. My mother, she just sat there, saying nothing. I'm not sure what hurt worse, her silence or my dad running his mouth in the heat of the moment. Anyways, I wasn't going to stay where not only was I not wanted but you weren't either. So, yeah, as far as tomorrow morning, or this morning, I guess, I'm not really sure what time it is right now, it might not happen. I'm really sorry, Wolf. So, so sorry." I'm wringing my fingers together, hair falling out of my messy bun, covering my eyes.

"Well, there's nothing to be sorry about. Shit happens. Time to get to bed though, sunshine. Daylight will be here before you know it. Nothing we can do about it now. May as well let everyone sleep on it and then go from there." He cups my cheek, bringing my eyes to his. God, this man, he's indescribable, and he's all freaking mine.

"Okay, thank you, Wolf, and I don't know if you've named the newest addition out there, but I'm pretty sure Dominic would be the perfect name for him." I smile at him.

"Is that right? Well, it's a good thing that's your donkey. I am thinking you've listened to one too many Christmas songs." He arches an eyebrow, and paired with his grin, I'm freaking toast. Panties wet, nipples pebbled, and my mouth is salivating for another taste of him.

"Who, me?" I tease back. Wolf doesn't mention anything else, instead, his lips meet mine, conveying everything I need to feel without another word, and I couldn't be more grateful.

FIFTEEN
WOLF

I NEVER THOUGHT I'd be doing this. Fuck, if it were anyone else, I probably would have blown them off and said to hell with this shit. But after an early morning with the animals, a call to my mom, I'm now standing on the doorstep of what had my woman silent and in my arms last night. The tears that slowly traveled down her cheeks, landing on my chest, sure as fuck didn't help. I knew talking about it wasn't going to help, so instead, I held her closer to me, not saying a word, silently comforting her. It kept me up even after she fell asleep. Hell, I don't think I caught an hour of shuteye.

"Can I help you?" My hand is at the ready to knock on the door, but it opens before that happens.

"Hi, you must be Mr. Miller. I'm Wolf Shaw." I hold my hand out, offering to shake his. Reese said her dad is old school, so I'm assuming he'll shake my hand.

"Hello, Reese mentioned you last night. I would have thought she'd be with you since she left so abruptly." He swiftly shakes my hand and then folds his arms over his chest, widening his stance.

"She's at my place, sir. Sleeping. I figured I'd take this time to introduce myself, allow you to see where we're coming from, and hopefully come to a truce." I keep my hands to my sides, loose, even though they're aching to ball into fists.

"Come in, may as well not have this conversation on the front porch. I'm not saying I'm enthused with how things are heading and so fast, but I can see that I've upset my daughter." I don't acknowledge that statement, knowing full well you don't rub salt in a wound.

"I'm hoping we can sort things out before she wakes up, though with Dominic at the house, it might keep her pre-occupied for a bit longer." His eyebrows move up to his hairline.

"Sorry, let me elaborate. Reese mentioned the ranch needed pigs and donkeys. A donkey was the best I was doing," I try to lighten things up as I step inside, smelling traces from Reese staying here, even though the majority of her things are tucked away back home.

"That girl always did have a thing for pets. She brought home so many stray pets, cats, dogs, turtles, and one time a snake." A woman who looks so much like Reese walks into the room. I instantly know it's her mom.

"Sounds like her. I'm Wolf. It's nice to meet you, Mrs. Miller." I offer my hand once again. Instead of shaking it, she squeezes my upper arms and kisses my cheek. That was the last thing I expected after Reese mentioned she was statue still while her dad laid into her.

"It's nice to meet you too. Sorry you're getting wrangled into this. My husband and daughter are two birds of a feather. Of course, I can't say that I wasn't apprehensive because I was and still am. After a long night, worrying sick over my obstinate headstrong girl, I should know she knows what she wants. And Joe here knew she's been miserable at her job. Haven't you, Joe?" Mrs. Miller busies herself in the kitchen, leaving us in the open concept living room that allows you to see where she went.

"Yeah, not real proud of the words that were said. I figure you showing up here, though, it shows us what kind of man you are. Well, depending on how everything is handled. One day, you'll understand if you have a daughter of your own. I just don't want her to come home, penniless, without a home, and heartbroken." He grabs the newspaper, shuffling it in his hands. The front door banging open has us all turning our heads.

"Momma, Daddy, Wolf." No hey, hi, or hello leaves Reese's lips when she barges through the door. I haven't seen Reese spitting mad. We've had one argument, and that ended up in make-up sex. Something tells me that won't be happening this time around. I'm just not sure who's she's more upset with, her parents or me. And if it's me, why she'd be spitting mad.

"Sunshine, come here." Trying to defuse the situation before worse things are spewed, I watch as she stomps her feet but still comes to me. My arm wraps around her shoulder, pulling her into my side, I kiss her temple and say, "It's alright, breathe through this. Your dad seems like he may want to talk."

"Whelp, looks like that apology you wanted to give her is at the station. Wolf, why don't you and I make breakfast and let these two have their talk. Then I need to trade spaces and do the same." Thankfully, Reese's parents seemed to have settled down some and don't want to argue again. I'm not sure I can take another night of my woman attempting to sleep away from me, then get upset, drive home, and wind up sleeping in the barn again.

"Well, okay, then." The frustration has seemingly left Reese, her body deflating against mine. As if she's bone deep tired, which is probably the case. A rough night, only to cry herself to sleep, then wake up and be here in the morning. Yep, I'm thinking once things are worked out, I'll be taking my woman home. Reese will get some kind of rest even if I have to wear her out.

"If you need me, just look my way. Give your dad a bit of understanding though. What if we were in their shoes? I'm not saying it was right, but I am saying that maybe it has some merit to it." She wraps her arms around my middle, squeezing me tightly and placing a kiss over my heart.

"Thank you. I'm still not happy you left without waking me up, but we can discuss that later on." I see the glimmer in Reese's eyes. Yeah, I know just what she wants, and I'm more than willing to give it to her.

SIXTEEN
REESE

IT'S awkward once Wolf leaves the room. This brings me back to a few childhood discussions where my father and I would butt heads and Mom would leave the room. We are both too stubborn to start a conversation or apologize. One thing is for sure, I'm not going to be the first one to do that today. I know he only wants what's best for me, but sometimes that means letting go and allowing me to spread my wings.

"I know you're upset. We're both allowed to be. I may have said things in the heat of the moment I'm not proud of, but you're my baby girl. My only child. Letting go is not easy. You up and moving down here with a man after you just recently met. It makes an old man weary. I will say I'll give credit where credit is due. Him bucking up and coming over without you, that says a lot about him. Forgive me, pumpkin?" Shit, he used the big guns, went for broke and called me pumpkin. I'm toast when he uses that nickname. That and the semi-apology, totally like my dad. It's hard to stay pissed off at him, plus I really want him and Wolf to get along.

"You know I can't stay mad at you long, but you hurt me,

Daddy. I appreciate your apology, but you have to know I'm going to make my own decisions and you may not like some of them. There might be a time you'll need to pick me up when I'm crumbling. Though, I have to tell you, it may be too soon for some, I love him, Daddy. And not just a toes-in-the-water kind, it's more of a diving headfirst, plunging into love." My nerves are frayed. Telling my dad something I should have probably—okay, not probably but definitely—told Wolf first. Now, I'll be praying that he didn't hear that. Knowing him though, with his supersonic hearing, Wolf will know and be sure to have another surprise up his sleeve, kind of like Dominic.

"Kind of figured that out by the way you had no problem going right to him, and that little tidbit of information he thought only your ear could hear. Well, it was loud enough. Might want to work on that with him. If you do ever have children, they'll hear everything." And just like that, he's making me cry and laugh at the same time.

"Wolf is just Wolf. What you see is what you get. He's got a heart of gold. I mean, for goodness' sake, he bought a donkey because I mentioned the chickens and cows needed a friend. Mind you, this was when I thought he wasn't around. He's a good person, Daddy. I promise you, my heart didn't steer me wrong."

"I hear you, loud and clear, pumpkin. Let's go see what your momma has Wolf doing in the kitchen. Knowing her, we'll have a spread for breakfast, and do me a favor?" he asks.

"What's that?" His arm wraps around my shoulder as we walk towards the kitchen.

"Go easy on your momma. Don't mistake her silence for what it was. She didn't like last night one bit. Me with my mouth and you slamming out the door. I got more than an earful for my behavior, deserved every bit of it too." He nods his head, and I know he's right, but it still hurts.

"I'll take that into consideration." My eyes focus on Wolf. He's standing at the kitchen counter, his back to me, flipping pancakes. Those muscular arms of his that hold me when I'm falling apart. Wolf is in his everyday grey shirt, denim jeans, and boots, making me want to bypass this whole shebang, go home with him, and get us both sideways.

"Oh, goodie, my turn. Though, if you're not careful, I may just steal this handsome man of yours. You didn't tell me Wolf knew how to cook." Mom abandons cutting fruit beside him, grabs my hand, and walks me back to where I just came from.

"He's a man of many trades, Momma. You don't have to say anything. I know you don't like to get in the middle of when Dad and I start our bickering. It's not easy when you have two hardheaded family members with a side of drama queen," I joke, not wanting her to feel bad.

"Well, know that I'm sorry and I love you. Parents don't always say the right things or do it right. It comes from the heart though," she states.

"I love you. Now, are you ready to eat? Because I'm absolutely starving." It was a shitty situation, one that doesn't need to be talked to death. And actions speak louder than words, and it seems like both of my parents are willing to give Wolf a chance.

"Let's go eat, then." Wolf, my parents, and food, that's what today was meant to be all about.

SEVENTEEN
WOLF

THIS PAST MONTH has been one fuck of a learning curve between getting Reese settled down here permanently and making sure her parents were okay with what was going on between us, then Mom coming over while the Millers were at the house. I think seeing how Mom brought not only Reese but her parents as well into the fold eased a lot of their hesitations.

The icing on the cake, though, that would be this clusterfuck over the last few weeks of dealing with what was once a loyal bartender turned sideways. It caused me to be at the bar more often than not. Sometimes I'd be rolling into bed when it was time for her to be up and feeding the animals, her decision, not mine when it came to doing the chores. Reese would do the morning feeding, and I'd do the evening. There were times when she and Mom would come up to the bar, put on an apron, helping me out while I caught up on paperwork. Thank God today the new bartender is able to be out on his own and I'm able to be home at a reasonable fucking hour.

"Reese, sunshine, you in here?" I slide off my boots, placing them on the new rack that's been added. She's placed her stamp all over this house with pictures of us. It's now more of a home rather than a house it's ever been. Another shoutout to my mom, no less. All those shopping trips seem to be paying off, and it's not killing Reese to have any issues with spending money, even if it isn't hers. That argument happened a time or ten, but now that she's found a job here in town to start in the fall, it's not killing her to watch every single penny.

"In the back bedroom," I hear Reese's voice carry through the house, my feet moving me towards her. Wondering if she's started working on that room next. If I had it my way, we'd be turning it into a nursery soon. That will happen one day. We're on the same page in the way that we both want at least three or four children. The only snafu we're having is the timeline on when that will be happening.

"Mother trucker, tell me you did not bring that thing inside the house?" Reese looks up at me, holding up this tiny creature, pink in color, slightly fuzzy, with black spots.

"Who, me?" She bats her eyes at me, a serene smile on her face, and in her arms is a baby pig.

"Sunshine, you know it's not going to be able to stay inside the house, right?" I hate to break it to her, but there's no way a pig can stay indoors. Not with how big they get.

"Wolf, it's a wittle little baby, plus it's teacup size. It'll stay this little forever. Please?" Reese pleads with me.

"Where'd you find her?" I can tell it's a girl by the pink tutu she has the little munchkin dressed in.

"The farmers market. Can you believe it? The guy was giving them away. You're lucky she was the last one left. If I had gotten there any earlier, well, let's just say we would have had them all here." She's so damn proud of herself that I don't have the heart to be upset.

"It's a good thing I love you, sunshine. You know it's not sleeping with us, though, right? Because I draw the line at that."

"What about in our bedroom?" she tries to counter.

"No fucking way. If it were our own baby, absolutely. But not a pig." I'm shutting that shit down right here and now.

"Fine, but it'll be you who gets upset when I traipse out of bed in the middle of the night to let Piglet here go potty."

"Nice try. I'll get up with her if need be, but you'd still take her out regardless of if she's in our room or not. Has Dominic met her yet?" There are days I can still find her outside talking to the cows, chickens, and donkey. It seems now there'll be a pig added to the mix, much to my chagrin.

"Yes, but she didn't care too much for him. Of course, that could be because he tried to snack on her, crazy donkey." I watch as Reese puts Piglet in the round pen she has set up, patting her little body, cooing almost, and damn if this woman wouldn't make a perfect mother to our children.

"He'll have to get used to her. It'll just take time. Dominic probably thinks she's a toy." My arms wrap around her after she walks towards me.

"Probably. How was your day?" Reese's head tips up, looking at me.

"It was a day, better now that I'm home. Shower with me?" I don't wait for her to respond. Instead, my lips meet hers, and I take her mouth, devouring her taste, feeling her hands glide up to my shoulders, our tongues tangling with one another, and there's no way I'm letting her go. I have one thing on my mind, and that's getting Reese wet and naked.

EIGHTEEN
REESE

I KNEW by the possessive way Wolf took my mouth that I was going to be in for a delicious night. He wrapped me up around his body, bypassing our bedroom and heading to the master bathroom. The summer dress I'm wearing already has Wolf's hands gripping the cheeks of my ass, my wetness coating his fingertips that meandered to my slick center.

"Wolf," I moan against his lips, but I also want to get his attention.

"You need me, sunshine?" Wolf slides me down his body, letting me go in the process, and I watch as he yanks off his shirt, displaying his bare chest, lightly smattered with hair. My eyes watch his hands as he unbuttons his jeans, baring his hard, thick cock to me, and I can't believe the words that are about to come out of my mouth.

"You, I always need you, but tonight, I kind of want something different." I unclasp my bra, allowing it to slide down my arms, baring my breasts to Wolf's gaze.

"You gonna say the words, or am I just gonna take it, sunshine?" His jeans are off, and Wolf is prowling towards me.

I tease. This was my idea after all, and I really want to give both of us this memory, forever.

"Fuck, I'm not sure how I got to be so damn lucky, but I'm thankful as hell for it." I bend over, my hands leaving his hair, falling flat on the wall in front of me, and spread my legs further apart.

"We both are. Now, are you going to finally take me?" I sass back. I'm looking over my shoulder, biting my lower lip and shaking my ass at him.

"Sunshine, you're playing with fire, and you're about to feel the burn." His hand comes down on my ass cheek, only fueling said fire with it. Wolf moves in closer after, fisting his cock, sliding more lube up and down his length. The corner of my eye capturing his every movement.

"I'm ready for it." I feel the wetness of lube that he pours between the globes of my ass, my head turning back to the wall, his fingers never leaving my pussy. I swear Wolf is a master magician when it comes to how he works my body, never leaving me.

"Christ," I hear him murmur as the head of his cock breaches my entrance. I take deep breaths, allowing my body to get used to his invasion. The delicious burn has me pushing back against him.

"Don't stop," I plead.

"Work your pussy, sunshine. I'm going to need both hands to fuck this hot ass." As the words leave his lips, I keep one hand on the wall as leverage, the other sliding on top of his for the moment, loving this connection we have. And when his fingers leave my center, my own take over. Wolf's hands grab my hips, and he works my body like he never has before. It's all-consuming, illicit, forbidden, but in the best way possible. The water running down the sides of our bodies, the heavy panting, the moans leaving us. It's like we were made for one another.

"Take me, Wolf, please." I slide my panties down the length of my body, and by the time he gets to me, both of us are naked, bare skin against bare skin, needy, in a tangle of limbs.

"Oh, I will, sunshine. Turn the water on and get inside. I'm going to get something." Thankfully, I don't have to say it out loud, but he's been working me up to it every time we have sex, and the feeling is indescribable. I start the water before stepping in, yelping when the cold water hits me.

"You do that every time." Wolf's arm bands around my center, his body giving me warmth while the water heats up.

"Well, it does get your attention too." I look over my shoulder. His eyes are full of hunger, and in his other hand, hanging loosely at his side, is the bottle of lube. My body shivers in delight, knowing I'm finally going to feel him deeper than ever before.

"Reese, there's nothing you don't do that doesn't get my attention," he groans before taking my lips with his. The thickness of Wolf's cock is sitting between the cheeks of my ass. As our kiss deepens, he uses it to build up the sensation of what he's going to do.

"God, Wolf," I purr, our lips parting when I feel his hand that was banded around my waist cupping my pussy, two fingers working inside me. I'm lost in a blissful state, loving the way Wolf knows how to work my body, so much that when I hear the cap pop open, it doesn't even faze me. The rapture that's surrounding my being has my hands over my head, delving into Wolf's hair, gripping it for dear life. The only reason I know he's about to enter me is when he says, "Take a breath, sunshine, let me in." The head of Wolf's cock is at my entrance. I do as he says, his fingers still working at my center. I'm on the tip of my toes, wiggling back on him, when I lose my footing and land back on my heels, losing his cock as well.

"This might be more of a learning curve than we thought,"

"Wolf." My pussy clamps on my own fingers.

"Shit, you better get there. The way your ass is tightening on my cock, I'm about to come, sunshine." I work faster, the palm of my hand rubbing against my clit, and when one of his hands leaves my hip, trailing down to where my fingers are, joining me, I'm falling apart at the seams. Eyes shut tight, on sensation overload, and Wolf comes with me. I feel his cum jetting inside a place no other person has ever been before and I know it won't be the last time we come like this.

EPILOGUE
REESE

Six Months Later

"YOU DID GOOD, pumpkin. I'm real proud of you. So is your momma." We're at the reception of mine and Wolf's wedding. We probably would have flown the coop, a justice-of-the-courts style, but that wasn't going to fly when we brought it up to my parents and Wolf's mom. The adamant nos came out in a whirlwind of anger. So, we waited and planned our wedding. It was funny to see my dad get wound up at the thought of us living in 'sin' while we planned it. I guess the joke was on him.

"Thanks, Daddy." It was worth it, the waiting to be Mrs. Wolf Shaw. I'd do it over and over again. We even left a seat open for Wolf's dad next to where Julia sat, a picture of the three of them framed and in his seat. When Wolf saw what my momma and I did behind his back, a tear ran unchecked down his cheek. Of course, this was all seen from around the corner in the small church we said our vows in. And when I walked down the aisle to my now husband, my eyes watered the entire time, especially when we said our vows together. Our gaze never wavered, even when my voice quivered. Wolf held my hand the entire time.

I look over Daddy's shoulder. The McCray family is here, our neighbors, Creed, and the other neighbors, Rhett and his sister, Laney. We really are two lucky people to have their love surrounding us.

"Now, I'm not saying I need grandchildren, but your mother is hemming and hawing about them already. If it were up to me, though, I'd suggest you wait. You and Wolf have your whole life ahead of you. Take the time to enjoy it." If Momma heard him, she'd give him the look, the one a mother gives when you're in a restaurant and your child is acting up.

"May I cut in?" Wolf saves me from answering.

"Sure can. Thanks for taking care of my baby girl." My dad lets me go, brings Wolf in for that half man hug thing, and then I'm in my husband's arms.

"You know I'd have you barefoot and pregnant in a heartbeat, but if you want to wait, I'm good with that too. Besides, we have more than enough animals to tide us over." He winks at me. He's not wrong. I think between the two of us, we've brought home every stray or homeless animal.

"I can't believe I'm going to say this, but I'm agreeing with Dad. I'd like to take some time and enjoy us for right now," I respond.

"Then that's what we'll do." Wolf brings me in closer, planting a kiss on my forehead.

"I love you, Wolf Shaw. You complete the missing pieces of me." I sigh.

"I love you, Reese Shaw, more than life itself." We sway to the music.

EPILOGUE
WOLF

Six Years Later

"DADDY, CAN WE ADOPT A GOAT?" Our daughter, Emmylou, is just like her momma. I mean that in all ways possible. She has Reese's personality, her looks, and definitely the same facial expression when she really wants something.

"Well, baby girl, that depends. Did your momma and mawmaw already bring it home?" I barely had my truck in *Park* after working at the bar today when she came barreling out of the house, dress flapping in the wind with her hair braided to one side like she asks Reese for every day.

"Emmy, baby, you weren't supposed to ask just yet. You at least need to wait until Momma says hello," my mom jokes with her. I guess that's my answer. These three women, with a side of Reese's mom, I never stood a chance.

"So, can we, Daddy?" Her hands are clasped together while she's jumping around and sticking out her bottom lip.

"I think it'll cost you. What do you say, a hug around my neck and a kiss on the cheek?" I tease her. I already knew this would happen. Thankfully, we have enough room for a few more animals. If we get too many more though, we'll have to look at buying some surrounding land.

"Thank you, Daddy, you're the very best." She jumps up. I pick her up, holding her to me, cherishing these moments, knowing my years with her thinking I'm the best there is will be numbered.

"Well, it's a good thing you're my best girl." I kiss the top of her head, soaking up her scent, crisp sunshine with a hit of hay.

"Did I miss all the fun again?" Reese comes out of the house, hair down in soft waves, sundress on, shoulders kissed by the sun, and barefoot. That's what happens when you're seven months pregnant and it's so hot here in Texas that all you want to do is plant your body in the closest body of water. Which has me conjuring up all kinds of ideas.

"Nope, but I heard we're now owners of a goat." I tickle Emmylou, causing her to laugh, before placing her on the ground.

"Well, you know how it goes. We just bring them all in. Though this will probably be it for a while. I'm afraid we'll need to have a petting zoo if we add another one." My woman, she's so full of shit. I give it another six months until another animal will wander into our home. Never mind the teacup pig that was supposed to stay as small as a football. Piglet ended up growing to be over one hundred pounds. Needless to say, she's out in the pasture with the cows and Dominic, the donkey.

"We'll see about that. Is Emmylou staying with you tonight, Mom?" I ask, walking towards her, planting a kiss on her cheek, then going to Reese.

"Oh yes, Daddy. We're going to watch movies, paint our nails, and eat all kinds of junk food." One thing about it, when these women get together, they conjure up all kinds of things. Though, I'm not going to complain about tonight, an evening to ourselves, one where I can make my woman come over and over again.

"How ya doin', sunshine?" My hand touches her swollen belly, our boy kicking me as I do so.

"I'd be better if you'd kiss me already," she smarts back with a smile on her face.

"Is that so?" I swoop down, taking her lips with mine. My tongue sneaks out, tangling with hers, savoring her flavor, and in the background, we hear Emmylou say, "Ewwww, Momma and Daddy are gross. Maw-maw, can we leave?" God, this life is fucking amazing. Something tells me it's only going to get better.

WHAT'S NEXT?

Did you enjoy seeing Creed? His story is coming next in Hotter, here's a sneak peek just for you!
Amazon

Laney

THEY SAY if you love someone to let it go, apparently a certain man named Creed took that to heart. That or he's a coward and ran away. I'm more inclined to think it's the latter with the way after he took me one hot summer night. I still remember it like it was yesterday, both of us stripping one another out of clothes, and when I saw him standing in front of me without so much as a piece of fabric on his long and lean body, it had me running towards him. Creed's mouth met mine, whimpers left my throat when he picked me up, my core sliding along the length of his cock, and when he brought me to the ground our lips never parting, it was amazing. The best part though was when he sunk inside me, nothing between us, not a care in the world. Not that he was ten years my senior or any type of protection was being use. It was just us and it was indescribable the amount of pleasure he brought me.

The next morning, Creed was a completely different person, tangled limbs, bare skin, and a sweet smile plastered on my face. He woke up, eyes bleary from sleep and the morning sun saying it was a mistake, that I was his best friend's little sister, and a slew of other excuses I refuse to even bring up.

That's why now that he's back home after being gone for nearly a year I'm not sure if I want to hug him or throttle him. It's been months and I've been radio silent to him. No matter how many texts or phone calls I received from Creed. He'll never realize that when he left how painful it was or when I cried that first month that my period came after secretly hoping we'd created a life together. I couldn't do it, I'm not even sure how I'll look him in the eye now. I sucked it up, because cowgirls don't cry.

Too bad watching your brother struggle even when you work beside him twelve hours a day is a hard pill to swallow. No one thought daddy would be forced to retire at such a young age, a stroke will do that though. Seeing our father try his best to get better day in and day out with little no avail, my heart broke for him and our mom who never leaves his side.

I know they say things come in three's and it sure seems like the Spencer family is seeing that happen this year, I'm just praying the third strike doesn't come from bringing back a certain man.

I definitely didn't think I'd have to suck it up and make a phone call I absolutely dreaded after dodging texts and calls for as many months as I could remember. My wounded pride was put to rest though, we were struggling, the horse farm came before self-importance. Rhett even hired a few extra hands, but it seemed like we'd train them to help then they'd leave at the drop of the hat. Not that this is an easy job for anyone and working for Rhett can be a nightmare of epic proportions, but we paid better than most. I couldn't understand it, neither could Rhett. So, we just stopped hiring people and took over the workload until I was bone tired, in tears, and so sore that even a hot bath wasn't helping.

When Creed picked up on the first ring, tears gathered in my eyes, emotion clogged my throat and I pleaded for help. He didn't hesitate, telling me he'd be home within two weeks and to try and do our best until he got here. Creed was meant for bigger things and even now I feel horrible for calling him home but I can't do this anymore. If it gets much worse, I'll be the one running away like Creed did and I can't do that to my family.

Amazon

JUST FOR YOU!

If you'd like a free ebook from me you can find it here!

Swept Away

SWEPT Away

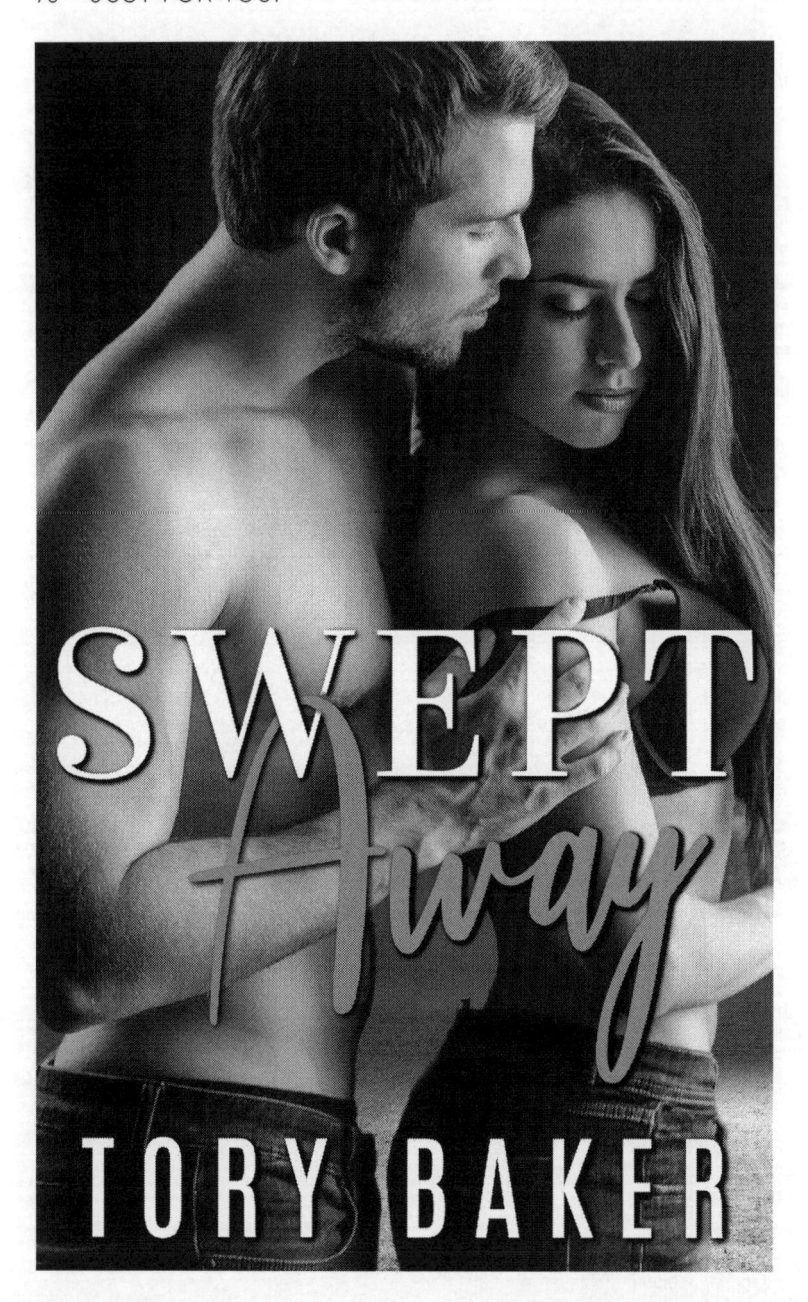

TORY BAKER

Tyler Banks stays busy running a successful bar. He loves his business, but his apartment is quickly becoming a dump. He contacts an agency and hires a cleaning lady, figuring it will be one less thing to worry about.

Little did he know the woman sent to clean up his mess would knock him on his ass.

Sutton Donnely is gorgeous and the way she fills out a white t-shirt and a pair of cut-off jeans should be illegal.

All it takes is one look and Tyler and Sutton are completely swept away in love.

Tory has a hot one for you. You met Tyler in Friend Zoned and now you get to see him find his one and only. As always with with a Tory book you're getting, a filthy talking alpha with insta-love galore and a sweet happily ever after to make you swoon!

ABOUT THE AUTHOR

Tory Baker is a devoted mother to her two children, who keep her busy with their abundance of energy and sports. She's a dog mom to her Weimaraner, Remi and her Beagle, Gunner. She lives in sunny Florida where she enjoys the sun, sand, and water anytime she can. Most of the time you can find her outside with a laptop on her lap, soaking up the rays while writing about Alpha men who love their women with everything they have to give and puts them first in everything they do with a guaranteed happily ever after.

Sign up to receive her **Newsletter** for exclusive giveaways and special offers.

Join her reader group, **Tory Baker's Readers** to be the first to look at new projects, fun giveaways, and more!

Follow Tory at:
Website - Facebook - Instagram - Bookbub - Goodreads

ALSO BY TORY BAKER

Bad Boys of Texas

Harder

Bigger

Deeper

Hot Shot Series

Fox

Cruz

Jax

Saint

Getting Dirty Series

Serviced (Book 1)

Primed (Book 2)

Licked (Book 3)

Hammered (Book 4)

Nighthawk Security

Never Letting Go (Easton and Cam's story)

Claiming Her (Book 1)

Craving More (Book 2)

Sticky Situations (Travis and Raelynn's story)

Needing Him (Book 3)

Only His (Book 4)

Carter Brothers Series

Just One Kiss

Just One Touch

Just One Promise

Finding Love Series

A Love Like Ours

A Love To Cherish

A Love That Lasts

Stand Alone Titles

Nailed

Going All In

What He Wants

Accidental Daddy

Love Me Forever

Gettin' Lucky

It's Her Love

Meant To Be

Breaking His Rules

Can't Walk Away

Carried Away

In Love With My Best Friend

Must Be Love

Sweet As Candy

Falling For Her

All Yours

Sweet Nothings Book 3—Tory Baker

Loving The Mountain Man

Crazy For You

Trick— The Kelly Brothers

Friend Zoned

His Snow Angel

223 True Love Ln.

Hard Ride

Slow Grind

Made in the USA
Coppell, TX
25 January 2025